Green Light Readers
For the new reader who's ready to GO!

Amazing adventures await every young child who is eager to read.
Green Light Readers encourage children to explore, to imagine, and to grow through books. Created for beginning readers at two levels of skill, these lively illustrated stories have been carefully developed to reinforce reading basics taught at school and to make reading a fun and rewarding experience for children and grown-ups to share outside the classroom.

The grades and ages within each skill level are general guidelines only, and books included in both levels may feature any or all of the bulleted characteristics. When choosing a book for a new reader, remember that every child progresses at his or her own pace—be patient and supportive as the magic of reading takes hold.

1 Buckle up!
Kindergarten–Grade 1: Developing reading skills, ages 5–7
- Short, simple stories • Fully illustrated • Familiar objects and situations
- Playful rhythms • Spoken language patterns of children
- Rhymes and repeated phrases • Strong link between text and art

2 Start the engine!
Grades 1–2: Reading with help, ages 6–8
- Longer stories, including nonfiction • Short chapters
- Generously illustrated • Less-familiar situations
- More fully developed characters • Creative language, including dialogue
- More subtle link between text and art

Green Light Readers incorporate characteristics detailed in the Reading Recovery model used by educators to assess the readability of texts through the end of first grade. Guidelines for reading levels for these readers have been developed with assistance from Mary Lou Meerson. An educational consultant, Ms. Meerson has been a classroom teacher, a language arts coordinator, an elementary school principal, and a university professor.

Published in collaboration with Harcourt School Publishers

Why the Frog Has Big Eyes

Betsy Franco

Illustrated by Joung Un Kim

Green Light Readers
Harcourt, Inc.
San Diego   New York   London

www.harcourt.com

First Green Light Readers edition 2000
Green Light Readers is a registered trademark of Harcourt, Inc.

Library of Congress Cataloging-in-Publication Data
Franco, Betsy.
Why the frog has big eyes/Betsy Franco; illustrated by Joung Un Kim.
—1st Green Light Readers ed.
p. cm.
"Green Light Readers."
Summary: A fable explaining how a staring contest left frogs with large eyes.
[1. Fables. 2. Frogs—Fiction.] I. Kim, Joung Un, ill. II. Title.
PZ8.2.F68Wh 2000
[E]—dc21 99-50805
ISBN 0-15-202536-7
ISBN 0-15-202542-1 (pb)

A C E G H F D B
A C E G H F D B (pb)

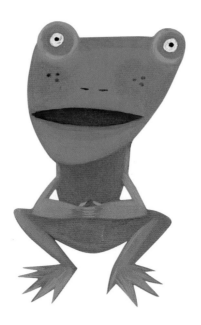

Long ago, all frogs had small eyes.

One frog sat and stared all day.

"No one can stare as long as I can,"
Frog bragged.

His friends said, "Let's stop his bragging.
Who can stare as long as Frog can?"

Horse trotted in.
"You will blink first," said Frog.
"I will not!" said Horse.

"See!" shouted Frog. "You did!"

Rabbit hopped in.
Rabbit didn't last long.
He blinked first.

"No one is better than I
am!" bragged Frog.

Fish flopped up.
"Frog will blink first this time!"
said Fish.

Fish stared at Frog.
Frog stared at Fish.
Fish didn't blink.
Frog's eyes got big, *big*, BIG.

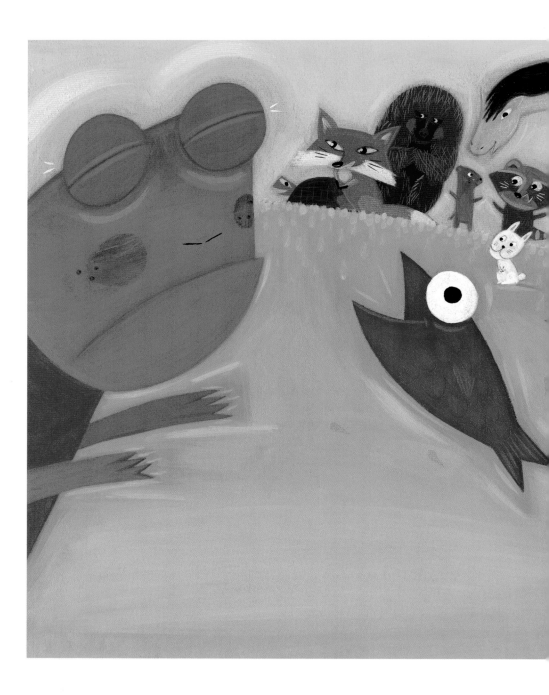

"Frog blinked!" shouted Fish. "Frog, a fish can't blink! Ha! Ha!"

Frog sat still.
His big eyes stared from that day on.

He didn't brag again.

Meet the Illustrator

Joung Un Kim visits bookstores and museums to get ideas for her drawings. She likes to try new things. For the story **Why the Frog Has Big Eyes,** *she practiced drawing animals. This is the second animal story she has illustrated.*